"Of all the works this great man and artist has written,

his short stories have made the strongest impression upon me.

I regard them as the most perfect tales ever written."

—Elisabeth of Wied, Queen consort of Romania (1881–1914)

"The Russian great was considered mad by some and a genius

by others. He was a radical and a saint. A noble-turned-ascetic

wanderer. No wonder so many were fascinated with

his life and stories."

—Writing Gooder, a blog of the Young Writers Society
for teenagers and young college students

"One of Tolstoy's greatest gifts—and also a source of torment—

was his addiction to the question of the meaning of life. He

never ceased asking himself why and how he should live, and

what was the point of all his money and fame."

—Roman Krznaric, cofounder of The School of Life in London;
author of *How Should We Live?*

"As in the most abstract of narrators, what counts in Tolstoy is

what is not visible, not articulated."

—Italo Calvino, twentieth-century Italian novelist and
short story writer

THREE SIMPLE MEN

& Other Holy Folktales

LEO TOLSTOY

THREE SIMPLE MEN

& Other Holy Folktales

RETOLD WITH NOTES AND INTRODUCTION
BY JON M. SWEENEY

ILLUSTRATED BY ANNA MITCHELL

PARACLETE PRESS
BREWSTER, MASSACHUSETTS

2015 First printing
Three Simple Men: And Other Holy Folktales
Text copyright © 2015 by Jon M. Sweeney
Illustrations copyright © 2015 by Anna Mitchell

ISBN 978-1-61261-586-8

Library of Congress Cataloging-in-Publication Data
Tolstoy, Leo, graf, 1828-1910.
  [Short stories. Selections. English]
  Three simple men : and other holy folktales / Leo Tolstoy ; retold with notes and introduction by Jon M. Sweeney ; illustrated by Anna Mitchell.
      pages cm
   Summary: "You've met the characters in these stories before. We meet them in folktales from all around the world. There is the simple, wise old man who understands far more than he knows; the pompous religious expert who discovers his folly before it's too late; nosey neighbors and petty relatives; and a fight between good and evil in which, by story's end, good and evil almost seem to switch places. These classic folktales, made popular a century ago by Leo Tolstoy, are retold here for a new generation, beautifully illustrated in this gorgeous book designed for reading out loud, reading over and over again, and giving to friends"— Provided by publisher.
   ISBN 978-1-61261-586-8 (paperback)
   1. Tolstoy, Leo, graf, 1828-1910–Translations into English. 2. Tales–Russia. 3. Religious fiction. I. Sweeney, Jon M., 1967- II. Mitchell, Anna, illustrator. III. Title.
   PG3366.A15S94 2015   891.73'3—dc23

10 9 8 7 6 5 4 3 2 1

Published by Paraclete Press
Brewster, Massachusetts
www.paracletepress.com

Printed in China

I SAID THAT I WAS SAVED FROM DESPAIR BY COMING TO SEE THE TRUTH.

—LEO TOLSTOY, FROM A LETTER WRITTEN TO HIS WIFE, SONYA,

December 1851

❦ CONTENTS ❧

INTRODUCTION

— xi —

THREE SIMPLE MEN

— 1 —

A GODSON
LEARNS TO FIGHT EVIL

— 13 —

ONE NEGLECTED SPARK
MAY BURN DOWN
A HOUSE

— 35 —

AUTHOR'S NOTES

— 55 —

ENDNOTES

— 60 —

A genuine work of art must mean many things. . . .
It is there not so much to convey a meaning
as to wake a meaning.

—GEORGE MacDONALD, *from his 1893 essay*
"The Fantastic Imagination"

E LIVE IN A TIME WHEN FAITH IS REDISCOVERING
the power of stories and storytelling. Stories
are, of course, what have always preceded
(and seeded) faith, but in most traditions, the living
communication of personal experience, narrative, images,
and spirituality was once too easily dampened by more
didactic forms of teaching. No longer.

Stories are where faith begins. Before there was Torah,
there were Jews telling stories, and then telling stories about
stories. Before there was Gospel, there was Jesus speaking in
parables and preaching by the Sea of Galilee, followed by his
friends telling other friends what they remembered hearing

Jesus say. So it is in every spiritual tradition. Stories create the tone, convey the message, communicate the character, and are the meaning of what becomes faith. Storytelling carries the day long before catechism is formed.

Stories are how a faith is renewed. Rarely are hearts moved by doctrine, but they are moved easily by stories that strike, like smoldering sticks on fresh kindling, sparking the flames of faith. Then, stories warm us. They illumine us. We see their light and we are able to imagine once again our lives participating in their ardor and glow.

Who are the storytellers? In the beginning, they were the first inspired ones. Who is the storyteller today? Inspired ones who are not supplanting, but supplementing, the work of priests, rabbis, and pastors. Storytelling is not sacramental or ritual work, but storytellers may be the primary conveyers of meaning and inspiration for the future.

The best thing you can do for your fellow, next to rousing his conscience, is—not to give him things to think about, but to wake things up that are in him; or say, to make him think things for himself.

So said George MacDonald in the essay on the imagination quoted above. That is how every great story is meant to pierce the hearts of its listeners/readers. Not coincidentally, Holy Scripture does this too. Surely that is why tales such as the three in this book are being rediscovered as we look for old/new ways of religiosity and faith today.

The tales we hear in the crib and the playroom stick with us throughout our lives. Those early stories can seem odd to us later in life, but their strangeness is also their genius. Mysteries of identity and personal boundaries begin taking shape when we hear "Goldilocks and the Three Bears." Vagaries of life and death are introduced to our imaginations by "Hansel and Gretel," in which an old woman ends up in an oven. And somehow it makes more sense to us as children than it does later as adults. This is one purpose of our oldest stories—folktales, fairy tales, and legends: to stimulate our capacities to understand what we will experience as we grow older.

There are those who choose to distinguish between fairy tales as creations of a fanciful imagination and folktales as somehow more rooted in history. But this is a false distinction and misses the essential point. They are all in one way or another a kind of fantasy (another frightful word, I realize, to some) and, as such, have the ability to communicate truth. One expert recently explained it this way: "The fundamental premise of fantasy is that the things it tells not only did not happen but could not have happened. In that literal untruth is freedom to tell many symbolic truths."[2]

There are plenty of fanciful elements in Tolstoy's folktales. I've chosen the stories in this volume because I believe there are certain truths they get at in ways that fantasy may best of all uncover. This is in contrast to how folktales are sometimes used in more outright pedagogical ways. Then, they lose their power. The more directly a story attempts to communicate, signaling rather than enabling the moral, the less effect it is likely to have upon readers. We're complex beings who process complexity well. That is what makes us human, and the simplistic tale forgets this.

So, the Tolstoy tales retold here fall somewhere between the classically indirect and the pedagogically obvious. I've deliberately excluded some of the ones he made most obvious, for they pack little punch. They don't accomplish what he might have hoped.

Tolstoy composed his versions of these stories after years of soaking up legends of his native Russia and beloved Russians in conversation. His biographers tell us how he often invited guests to Vasnaya Polyana, always to talk religion and philosophy, and how he listened carefully. He also famously revered and observed the lives of ordinary men and women, peasants and serfs, pondering why they seemed to be happy regardless of their station in life, lack of formal education, and often hapless circumstances. He listened to their stories most of all.

This was also the time in Tolstoy's life when he turned from the intellect (mostly Schopenhauer's philosophy) as his primary source of wisdom to the heart. He became interested in living a life of simple piety, modeling himself after the lives of ordinary Russians whom he knew in the countryside or who worked on his own rural estates, far from the life he'd previously thrived in, in St. Petersburg and Moscow. In 1870, the year after publishing his first masterpiece, *War and Peace*, the great writer reflected in his journal, "As soon as man applies his intelligence and only his intelligence to any object at all, he unfailingly destroys the object."[3] So he determined to make his faith simpler, based more on trust than doubt. Tolstoy deliberately quieted the intense religious and spiritual questioning that had characterized his previous life. Not that the questions ceased, but they were quelled by the greater movement of his heart, welling up around the passions, emotions, and practices of faith. Thus, by the late 1870s, he seems to have begun to know God personally.

His religious life, which had mostly lain dormant since childhood, restarted. Tolstoy began to attend Mass, take communion, and fast regularly, and he sought out his brethren rather than singling himself out from them. He learned from Pascal that religious practice, done faithfully and honestly, can create true faith where before there was only the struggle to reason oneself to God. He began to acknowledge that happiness and philosophical speculation don't usually go hand in hand, and that in the Gospels Christ praised the simple faith of children. As was often the case, Tolstoy expressed this in the strongest and most personal of terms: "If Christian teaching and love (which I hate, because it has become a pharisaical word) leads to people calmly smoking cigarettes and going to concerts and theatres and arguing about Spencer and Hegel, then the devil take such teaching and love."[4] Faith and happiness well from the heart, and Tolstoy wished for that grace.

Conversion in Tolstoy's life was the prelude to his writing these tales. While publishing his second masterpiece, *Anna Karenina*, in 1877, the religious crisis was at its most intense. A sensitive reader can feel this in the final chapters of *Anna Karenina* itself. Tolstoy was seeking a more authentic, intimate relationship to God. Following that novel, these stories, composed in the 1880s, were part of the spiritual outpouring of his ever-renewing interior life. No one who knew him—or even saw him—during those years could mistake a spiritual passion inside of him. Tolstoy was, quite deliberately, in both his interior life and external appearance, very much a pilgrim.

It remains unclear how original Tolstoy's versions were and how much they were learned from others. Like all folktales, these three stories have a provenance that's ultimately impossible to trace. They originated in the lives of ordinary people and have been told innumerable times with all sorts of variances. But there is no question that an evangelical zeal accompanies them in their Tolstoyan forms.

They first became known to me through the English translations of the husband and wife team Louise and

Alymer Maude, who were also Tolstoy's personal friends. In the versions you are about to read, I've retold them further. Once a story takes hold of you, it doesn't let go easily, and the Tolstoy-Maude versions have had that impact upon me for the last thirty years, since I first read them in my late teenage years. I've lived closely with them since that time, often retelling them in conversations with friends and acquaintances, in situations where I have been "working out" my own spiritual issues and priorities. In other words, the oral roots of these stories keep on resisting immutability!

To quote Philip Pullman, who recently created fresh versions of fifty tales from the Brothers Grimm, I asked myself, "How would I tell this story myself, if I'd heard it told by someone else and wanted to pass it on?"[5] It is in that spirit that these new versions of three stories I have loved have been created. Details as to what I've changed, expanded upon, and deliberately diminished from Tolstoy's versions may be found in the Author's Notes at the back of this book.

May more readers find these stories, as I once did, for the first time.

THREE SIMPLE MEN

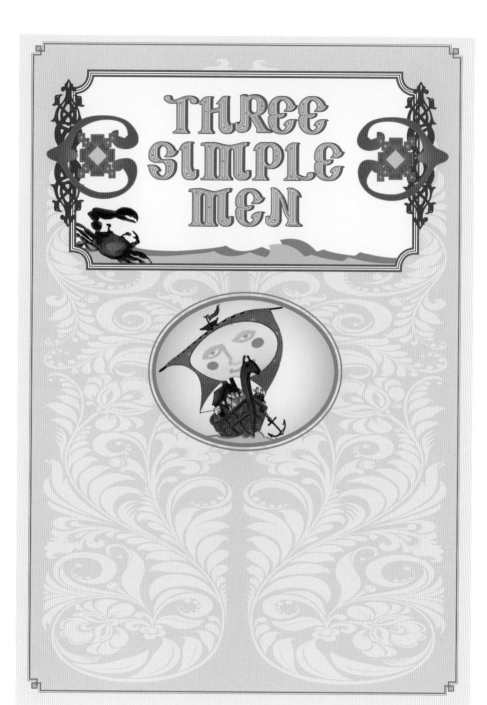

Three simple men lived on a small island in the middle of a great sea.

THREE SIMPLE MEN

 HREE SIMPLE MEN LIVED ON A SMALL ISLAND
in the middle of a great sea. They'd lived
there, together like brothers, for as long
as anyone could remember.

Each man possessed a long beard that reached almost
down to his knees. Each also had a special job he performed
as a prayer to God, and to help his friends.

The littlest man was a basket maker. They kept their food
in baskets, hanging them high in the palm trees to keep away
from the animals—from all but the monkeys, that is. Baskets
were also their beds, hung like hammocks. So the men
needed lots of baskets. The little man's shoulders hunched
from the long hours it took to make each one, but he was

always smiling. "Thanks be to God," he'd whisper when one of his baskets turned out especially fine.

The strongest man was in charge of finding food. He didn't smile as naturally as the littlest man, but he worked hard and was generous. He hiked all over the island, climbing every kind of tree in search of bananas, papayas, almonds, mangoes, and oranges. "God's bounty!" he would loudly call out each day while carrying large armfuls of food back to the house.

The tallest man was a thinker. He seemed to always be thinking about something important. His chin was often in his hand and wrinkles spread across his forehead. He liked to solve problems, and whenever the three men needed to figure out a new way to do something, the tallest man would ponder it thoroughly and come up with the best solution.

These three simple men lived together in a hut made of dark earth and native grasses. The sea surrounded them like sparkling blue-green glass. They were happy on their island home.

One summer day, two young priests were on a ship traveling from the city of Arkhangelsk, the chief northern port of Russia, to Solovki Monastery in the islands of the White Sea. Their ship hung low in the deep waters, so packed was it with Christian pilgrims traveling to see the legendary monastery. Their voyage was smooth and the weather on their journey, fine.

Late one afternoon, as they passed close by one of the small islands en route to Solovki, the young priests were on deck admiring the setting sun when they saw three simple men together on a faraway beach. They were surprised that anyone could live in such an out-of-the-way place so far from civilization. In fact, they were shocked to see any human beings at all on such a remote island! So they asked the captain of the ship to stop.

Immediately the captain set to halting the ship's course, but before he could drop the anchor offshore, the two priests, impatient to set foot upon the island, splashed into the water and were drenched by the time they reached the sand.

There, on the beach, three simple men greeted the priests by bowing deeply as they approached.

There, on the beach, three simple men greeted the priests by bowing deeply as they approached.

"Hello!" one of the priests called out, and then, "We have been sent by our bishop to teach people without God how to know him.

"Tell me, good men, do you desire to know Christ?"

The three men remained silent. The priests did not know if they understood the words they were speaking.

"Oh . . . excuse us," the other priest began to say. "Do you speak our language? Can you . . . understand us?

"Tell me, how do you good men pray?"

The tall man rubbed his forehead, glanced at his two friends, and replied, "We always pray, 'We are three, praise to Thee, have mercy on us.'" When he finished saying these words, the other simple men looked pleased. They all lowered their eyes and repeated quietly together, "We are three, praise to Thee, have mercy on us."

"Oh no. That is incorrect," the first priest said. "Dear friends, we can show you the right way to pray."

Then the priests began to explain many complicated things to the simple men. They talked for a long time about God, true faith, and the holy catechism, and while they talked the three simple men stood silently, listening. The little man smiled, the strong man looked very kind, and the tall man looked quite serious.

Finally, the first priest said, "God wants us to pray this way: 'Our Father, who art in heaven, hallowed be Thy name.' Good men, repeat that after me, please."

"This is just the beginning," added the second priest.

The men were visibly confused. They stood silently, looking at each other. Then the tall man made an attempt. "Our Father, who cart to bevan . . ." he said, until he realized that what he was saying sounded wrong.

The little man and the strong man tried to pick up the prayer where their friend had left off, but they too blundered the words, even worse than the tall man had done.

"Stop!" the priest called out. "My good men, what is wrong with you?

"*Now* . . . try again," he firmly but quietly commanded.

The men were stymied. They didn't want to offend their visitors and yet they couldn't seem to form the words their visitors were teaching them. They were simple men. So they began to ask questions. Was their own prayer wrong? How did one pray these new words? What did they mean?

The priests only grew more impatient. "You need to simply pray this way, my friends," the first priest exclaimed.

So the simple men began to pray again, anxious to make the priests happy. They lowered their eyes and repeated quietly in unison, "We are three, praise to Thee, have mercy on us." Then they prayed their prayer together again. While they repeated their words over and over, the little man smiled, the strong man looked very kind, and the tall man looked quite serious.

"Uh oh!" the tall man realized, when they were nearly done. They'd done it incorrectly again.

This went on for quite some time. The young priests tried to fix the prayers of the simple old men, to no avail.

Eventually the moon was rising on the horizon and the priests needed to return to their ship. As they were leaving, the second priest asked the simple men to please practice the prayer they had tried to teach them. "God will hear you when you pray this way," he reminded them.

Under a sky full of stars, the three simple men bowed deeply as the priests' ship set back out to sea. The water was glimmering with the reflection of a full white-orange moon.

The priests stood on the ship's deck, looking back at the island as they sailed away. They talked about how those simple men needed to learn the ways of God, and they wished to each other that the men had listened and learned more effectively.

Suddenly, the ship's captain looked across the water. "Ho! Starboard!" he yelled, piercing the quiet of the midnight waters. "What the devil is *that*!"

The ship's crew rushed to the side of the ship, looking intently toward the horizon. The young priests came close to look as well, and the crew separated to make room for them near the bow. Moonlight was glowing upon the water. And as priests and crew looked they saw something moving over the waves toward the ship. They saw what looked like the three simple men approaching!

There they were, running swiftly and steadily on top of the water toward the priests' departing vessel.

"Lower the anchor . . . *immediately*!" the captain yelled, and the ship soon came to a stop on the open sea.

The simple men grabbed ropes lowered by the dumbfounded crew and one by one they climbed aboard.

Walking directly over to the two priests, they bowed deeply, as they had before, on the beach. The tall man stepped forward.

"We are so sorry," he began. "We have forgotten the prayer you taught us. Will you please teach us once more?"

The priests could not speak. The first priest lowered his eyes, pressing his palms together. The second priest reached out his hands toward the simple men. After a few seconds, he said, "Friends, you need no instruction. Please pray as you have. And please pray for us."

With this, the little man said, "Thanks be to God," and as he began to pray his brothers joined him:

We are five, praise to Thee, have mercy on us.

Quietly, the simple men climbed back down the side of the ship and made their way across the water, just as they had come.

[JESUS SAID,] "WHEN YOU ARE PRAYING, DO NOT HEAP UP EMPTY PHRASES AS THE GENTILES DO; FOR THEY THINK THAT THEY WILL BE HEARD BECAUSE OF THEIR MANY WORDS. DO NOT BE LIKE THEM, FOR YOUR FATHER KNOWS WHAT YOU NEED BEFORE YOU ASK HIM."

—MATTHEW 6:7–8 NRSV

A GODSON LEARNS TO FIGHT EVIL

*The godson picked up a tool from the floor of the forbidden room and
hurled it at the murderer with all his might. . . .*

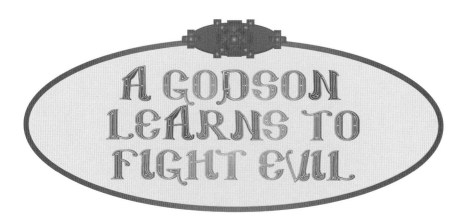

A GODSON LEARNS TO FIGHT EVIL

 HERE ONCE WAS A PEASANT WHO WISHED dearly for a son. Year after year he asked God to grant him such a blessing, until one day, his wife bore him a boy. Delighted, the very next day this peasant went next door to ask his neighbor if he would consent to being the boy's godfather. The neighbor flatly refused. "I don't want to be godfather to any poor man's child," he said.

So the peasant asked another neighbor. He also refused. Then our peasant walked door to door in his village, knocking on every one, seeking a godfather for his baby boy. But he found no one willing.

"I will simply go to the next village," he said aloud to himself, undismayed and without disappointment. He set out for the highway. And before he had taken five steps, the peasant met a stranger on the road.

"Good day, my good man," said the stranger. "Where are you headed?"

"God has given me a child," the peasant replied, still undeterred, "but I am a poor man and no one in our village will stand as his godfather. So now I am off to seek a godfather elsewhere."

"I will do it," said the stranger without pause.

The peasant was pleased but also taken aback. He paused for a moment, smiled broadly, and then pondered out loud, "Good! But who will be the godmother?"

"Go to the next village," the stranger offered. "In the square you will see a stone house with shop windows in front. Ask the man who answers the door if you may speak with his daughter, for she is to become the godmother to your child."

The peasant hesitated, again surprised.

"How can I do that?" he asked the man. "Who is this woman?"

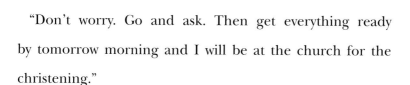
"Don't worry. Go and ask. Then get everything ready by tomorrow morning and I will be at the church for the christening."

So the poor peasant went straight to the next village, looking for the tradesman's house in the square. He'd hardly taken his horse into the man's yard when the man stepped out of his front door. "What do you want?" he demanded of the peasant.

"Why, sir . . . you see . . . God has given me a son! He brings me joy. He will comfort me in my old age, and he'll pray for my soul after I am gone," said the peasant. "Please, will you be so kind as to allow your daughter to be his godmother?"

"When is the christening?" the tradesman asked.

"Tomorrow morning," said the peasant.

"Fine. Go, then. You must have plenty to do to get ready. My daughter will be with you at Mass tomorrow morning."

The following morning the godmother came, the godfather came, and the peasant's son was baptized. Immediately following the service, the godfather vanished. None of them knew who he was.

T W O

This christened boy grew up a joy to his parents, as the peasant knew he would. He was strong, clever, and obedient. When the boy turned ten, his parents sent him to school, and what other children learned in five years he learned in only one. Soon there was nothing more his teachers could teach him.

One Easter, with the blessing of his parents, the boy went to see his godmother to give her his Easter greetings. "Now, father and mother," he said, returning home again, "where does my godfather live, so that I may also give him my love?"

"We don't know," the peasant replied. "Since the day you were baptized we have never seen him or known a thing about him. We don't even know if he's alive."

The boy bowed to his parents and said, "Well, then, father and mother, let me go and look for my godfather. I *must* find him."

What could they do? His parents let him go.

THREE

After walking for several hours, this determined godson met a stranger on the road traveling in the opposite direction.

"Good day to you, my boy," the stranger said. "Where are you headed?"

The godson answered, "I seek my godfather, kind sir. No one knows where he has gone or what has come of him."

"I am your godfather," replied the stranger.

Surprised, the godson immediately embraced the man, kissing him three times, in the customary Easter greeting. Then he said, "Which way are you going, godfather? If you are traveling in our direction, come to our home and stay. If you are going to your own home, let me come with you."

"I cannot just now," said the godfather, "for I have business to attend to. But I will be home tomorrow. Come and see me then."

"How will I find you?"

"When you leave home, go straight toward the forest. Walk through it until you find a garden. You may walk for a long time, but you will eventually find my house in the garden, with a golden roof. I will meet you at the gate."

With that, the stranger was gone.

FOUR

The godson did just as his godfather told him, and the following day he was welcomed at the gate of the golden-roofed house in the midst of the garden, at the farthest end of the forest.

The godfather showed the boy inside, and the boy marveled at the beauty of the place. Every room was like a palace, more splendid than the last. But then they came to a door in the house that was sealed shut.

"Look at this door, my son," the godfather said, "and remember it, because you are forbidden to enter here." That is all he said. Then the godfather went away.

Before long, the godson had trouble heeding the advice of his godfather. He opened the seal on that forbidden room and walked inside. Once inside, he saw all sorts of things that were new to him—especially the ways that people did evil in the world. He saw a thief stealing sheaves of corn from a neighbor's field early one morning before the sun was up. He saw a man secretly leaving his wife's bed in order to flee to his mistress. And he saw a woman murdered at the hand of a man who broke into her home late at night. At this last sight, the godson picked up a tool from the floor of the forbidden room and hurled it at the murderer with all his might, killing the man on the spot.

FIVE

The moment the murderer died, the walls of the forbidden room closed around the godson and he was suddenly standing back in the hallway. At that moment, in walked his godfather.

"You disobeyed me," the godfather said, "and as a result, you have seen many things. You also have done terribly wrong.

"You have added to evil in the world. Now you must go and do what you can to rid the world of these things."

"But how can I destroy evil in the world?" the godson asked.

"Go out and walk through the forest. Travel until you come to a small thatched hut. That is the cell of a hermit. Tell him what you have seen and what you have done. He will teach you what to do next."

SIX

The boy went on his way, worried and wondering. *How can I possibly destroy evil in the world? Isn't evil destroyed by banishing and imprisoning evil people, or by putting them to death? What can I do?*

He walked for days until he finally found the hermit's cell in the middle of the forest. He knocked on the door.

"Who's there?" asked a voice from within.

"A sinner," replied the boy, and with that, the hermit came out. The godson told the old man everything that had happened, all that he had seen, and the evil he himself had done.

"I have seen that one cannot destroy evil with evil," said the boy, "but I don't understand how to really destroy evil. I was told that you might be able to teach me."

"Come," said the hermit, picking up an axe. They walked for a few minutes and stopped at an old apple tree.

"Cut it down," said the hermit. The boy whacked at it over and over again until it fell to the forest floor with a thunder.

"Now, chop it into three pieces," the hermit said. And the boy did so, while the hermit returned briefly to his cell in order to gather a few burning sticks from his fire.

"Now, burn those three pieces," said the hermit, handing him the burning sticks that he'd fetched. The godson made a fire, placing the three logs in the middle of the flames. Together, the two sat and watched the fire in silence until all three logs had become charred stumps.

"Plant them in the ground, like this," said the hermit, showing the boy what he meant, digging a hole with the heel of his foot and the help of a nearby stick, in order to place most of a charred stump into the fertile forest floor.

"When you are done, bring water from that stream over there, and pour it over these stumps."

The boy began to do so.

"Water them every day and you will see that each has taken root and new apple trees have sprung. Then, you will know how to destroy evil in others as well as in yourself."

SEVEN

The following day, the old hermit was dead. His heart grieving, the godson took a shovel and dug a deep grave, reverently burying the elder whom he'd known so briefly. When he was done, late that evening, the boy remembered to water the charred stumps once again. Then he went to bed in the hermit's cell.

The following morning, a few pilgrims showed up at the hermit's door. When they heard that the old man had died and saw that the boy was living in his cell, tending his fire, they knew that the hermit had blessed the godson and they added their own blessings, promising to bring the boy food from time to time and asking for his blessing in return.

Before long, the boy was regarded by the people of the province as the new hermit, a wise man, although young, who was carrying on the work of his elder. Pilgrims often came visiting from long distances, and wealthy merchants, too, bringing presents, which the boy gave away to the poor. All the while, he continued to water the charred stumps with what he gathered from the nearby stream.

The godson began to wonder if this was, in fact, how he was supposed to destroy evil in the world. For two years he lived this way, seeing pilgrims come and go, watering the stumps each day, and yet none of the stumps sprouted. Until one day the boy heard a man on a horse approaching. He stepped out of his cell to see who it was.

"Greetings," the godson said to the stranger. "Where are you headed?"

"I am no one," the man responded, drawing rein. "I ride about the highways killing people, and the more I kill, the merrier the songs I sing."

The godson was struck with horror as he listened to this frank non-confession. He wondered, *How can evil be destroyed in such a man as this?*

Then he said, "People visit me here to repent, pray for forgiveness, and consider a new path in their lives. Repent, if you fear God. But if there is no repentance in your heart, please don't trouble me, and go away."

The robber laughed.

"I'm not afraid of God or anyone. Live however you like. Teach your pieties to the little old women who visit you. You have nothing to teach me." And, with that, the robber rode away.

EIGHT

One evening at twilight, the godson went to water his stumps. While he stood before them, pouring water upon them, he began to wonder if his life was all it should be. He remembered how the robber had made fun of his pieties, and of the pilgrims who visited him. *The hermit gave me penance to do, and I have replaced that with feeling good about being praised by others for holiness,* he thought to himself. *Am I really so holy?*

So, the godson determined to leave his place, and to find another, deeper in the forest, where he could pray and fast and be known to no one. He filled a bag with dried bread, left the cell, and started for a ravine he knew, where he could dig a cave and hide from the people who often visited.

While he was on his way, the robber suddenly came upon him. "Where are you going?" the robber demanded of the godson. The boy told him the truth.

"But what will you live on, without pilgrims coming to see you?" the robber said.

"On whatever God pleases to give me," the boy replied. With that, the robber turned his horse's head and began to leave.

I should have reminded him of his sins, the godson quickly reproached himself. *I am a coward.* So he called out, "You still should repent of your sins! You know, you cannot escape from God!"

The robber turned his horse back around and, drawing a knife from his belt, held it up to the godson's pale white throat. The boy's eyes went wide. Then he scampered into the forest.

"Twice now I have let you go. But next time, if you come my way, I will kill you!" the robber yelled to the boy running away deep into the woods. And then the robber rode just as quickly in the other direction.

That evening, despite finding the ravine and beginning to prepare his new cave, the godson returned faithfully to water his stumps, and one of them was sprouting. A little apple tree was growing out of it.

NINE

The godson began to live all alone, hidden from everyone. But after a while, he ran out of bread and was very hungry. So, he left his cave in search of some roots and berries but, finding none, became discouraged until he spotted something hanging from a tree. It was a bag of bread. He thanked God, took it down from the branch, and returned to his cave.

The boy ate in his modest way, and the bread lasted a full week. Then the boy left his cave once again, and again he found a bag of bread on a nearby tree. Thus he lived and ate, but in fear of facing the robber who had threatened his life.

The boy sometimes thought he heard the robber and his horse passing nearby, and whenever that happened, he hid himself. This is how he lived for ten years deep in the forest, until he was no longer a boy but had grown to be a man. He faithfully watered the stumps each day, and, as yet, there was only one that had flowered, becoming a new tree.

I have now become afraid of death, the godson realized one day, *and surely this is wrong before God. I wonder if it is God's will that I should redeem my sins by death?* Hardly had this thought passed out of his mind when the godson heard the robber coming near, swearing loudly at something.

This time the boy went out to meet the robber on the path that ran through the forest. There the godson saw not only the robber but what appeared to be another man, bound and gagged, sitting behind the robber on the saddle. The godson put up his hand to the horse's nose, causing the animal to come to a full stop.

"Where are you taking this man?" the godson asked the robber.

"Deep into the forest. This is a rich merchant's son who won't tell me where to find his father's loot. I'm going to beat him until he does," the robber said, giving the man an elbow in the ribcage. The man let out a moan. Then, the robber jerked his horse to the side, preparing to bolt.

But the godson jumped into his path, grabbing hold of the bridle. He demanded, "Let the man go!"

The robber was incensed. Raising his arm to hit the godson across the face, he screamed, "Here! I'll give you a taste, boy!" But the godson didn't move an inch. He looked the robber in the eyes. He was unafraid.

"I won't let you go," the godson shouted. "I fear no one but God, and God wills that I not let you pass without setting this man free." His lip trembled just slightly.

With that, the robber lowered his fist and snatched up his knife. With one swift motion he cut the ropes holding the merchant's son firm, setting him free. "Get away, both of you!" he demanded. "And don't cross my way again!"

The merchant's son ran wildly into the forest. But the godson remained. He spoke to the robber gently about the need to give up his evil ways. The robber listened, quietly now, until he rode away without saying a further word. The next morning when the godson walked through the forest to water the stumps, he found that the second stump was sprouting.

TEN

Ten more years went by. The godson sat quietly, desiring nothing, fearing nothing, and possessing a heart full of joy.

One day, remembering all the evil that he had seen in the world up until that point, he thought to himself, *It is wrong for me to live as I do. I must go and teach others what I have learned.* At that very moment, he heard what sounded like the robber passing by in the forest once again.

It is no good talking with him, the godson thought. *I will let him go his way.*

But a moment later, the godson reconsidered and went out to the path that travels through the forest. He saw the robber approaching slowly on his familiar horse. They both looked downcast, the robber without the evil mirth that always seemed to animate him.

The godson approached both robber and horse. "Brother, have pity on your own soul," he said to the man. "In you lives the spirit of God. You bring suffering to others but God loves you and has prepared blessings for you. Change your life!"

The godson approached both robber and horse. "Brother, have pity on your own soul,"
he said to the man. "In you lives the spirit of God."

The robber only frowned and turned to go. "Leave me alone," he said.

But the godson held the bridle of the horse. And then the godson began to weep. The robber lifted his eyes to look in the godson's face. He saw the godson in tears.

"You have overcome an old man," the robber began, descending from his horse and falling on his knees. "When you hid your pieties from other people, I began to bring you bread. Then, when I saw that you didn't fear death, my heart began to turn. But it didn't soften—not until now, not until you wept for me."

Hearing this, full of joy, the godson led the robber to the place in the forest where the stumps had long been cultivated. When they arrived, they saw together how the third stump had just begun flowering into an apple tree. At last, it seemed, the boy had learned about evil and how to overcome it.

You have heard that it was said,

"An eye for an eye and a tooth for a tooth."

But I say to you, do not resist an evildoer. But if anyone

strikes you on the right cheek, turn the other also.

—matthew 5:38–39 nrsv

THE
END

ONE NEGLECTED SPARK MAY BURN DOWN A HOUSE

The daughter-in-law was offended. She responded, saying more than she should have.

ONE NEGLECTED SPARK MAY BURN DOWN A HOUSE

 VAN SHCHERBAKOV'S GRANDFATHER was an old man, ill with asthma. Every day he lay upon the brick stove in the center of their large house, the action of the world going on all around him. He observed everything, and he recognized folly when he saw it.

Ivan, meanwhile, was comfortably situated, in the prime of his life. The best worker in the village, he also had three able-bodied sons. The eldest was married, the second son was about to become so, and the third was a big boy who minded the horses and did much of the plowing. Ivan's wife was a thrifty woman, and they were fortunate to have a quiet, hard-working daughter-in-law to boot. In other words, there was nothing to prevent Ivan and his family from being happy. They had only one idle mouth to feed—the grandfather, and he'd been lying atop that stove, sick with asthma, for the better part of the last seven years.

Ivan had everything he needed: three horses and a colt, a cow with a calf, and fifteen sheep. The women made all the clothing for the family, besides helping in the fields, and the men worked the land. They always had the grain they needed, with plenty left over to sell in order to pay their taxes. Ivan and his family might have lived comfortably were it not for a feud that rose up between him and his neighbor, Gabriel, son of Gordey Ivanov.

When Ivan's father and Gordey were both alive, the two households behaved as good neighbors should. If a woman of the house was in need of a tub, or one of the men needed to mend a broken cartwheel, they could easily ask the other and receive assistance. If a calf strayed onto the neighbor's threshing floor, the neighbor would simply send it out again, back to its home. No one ever thought, in those

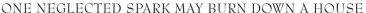

better days, of locking a barn, or hiding things, or telling tales about one another.

That was then. Everything changed soon after Ivan and Gabriel became the heads of their families.

It all began with a trifle. Ivan's daughter-in-law discovered that her hen was laying eggs rather early in the season, so she began collecting them for Easter. Every morning she found one egg, except on the fateful day when her hen, probably frightened by the children's playing, was not in its usual place. The daughter-in-law heard its cackling but thought to herself, *I don't have time just now. I'll find where she's left the egg later.* But when she looked that evening, she found no egg. She asked members of her family if they'd seen it. They hadn't. Then someone said, "I think your biddy laid its egg in the neighbor's yard. I saw her fly back across the fence when she was done."

The daughter-in-law went and looked at the hen. The biddy was sitting calmly on her perch beside the other birds, her eyes closing as if to go to sleep. Next, Ivan's daughter-in-law walked across to the neighbor's yard. There, Gabriel's mother came out to meet her. "What do you need?" the older woman said.

"I believe my hen flew across this morning. Did she lay an egg on your side?"

"We haven't seen anything," the woman responded. "Thanks be to God, our own hens started laying days ago. We collect their eggs and have no need for anyone else's. And we don't go looking in other people's yards!" Her tongue was unusually sharp.

The daughter-in-law was offended. She responded, saying more than she should have. Gabriel's mother then responded in kind. Soon Ivan's wife chimed in, as did Gabriel's wife, until bickering over one egg turned into "And you made a hole in the sieve I lent to you!" and "Why don't you ever give us back the yoke you borrowed?" Within ten minutes, the women were even swatting at each other. One of them then snatched off another's shawl.

At that moment the men arrived from the fields. Gabriel stood beside his wife. Ivan and one of his sons stood by Ivan's wife. And Ivan's grandfather, lying upon the brick stove inside the house, heard everything.

That was how it all began.

TWO

In the melee that morning, Ivan had apparently grabbed Gabriel's beard, pulling out a handful of hair. The following day, Gabriel gathered the hair, wrapped it in paper, and took off for the district court. Gabriel's wife whispered to some of the other neighbors, "We'll have Ivan condemned and sent to Siberia."

Inside Ivan's house, the grandfather asked his family to stop and reflect. "What foolishness," he said, from atop his stove, "picking fights over a simple egg. One stupid egg! One of the children could have taken it—did you consider that? Besides, what is the value of a single egg? God provides enough for all of us."

"And suppose your neighbor said an unkind word to you," the grandfather went on. "Fine. Put it right. Show her how to say a better one! And suppose that you had a bit of a fight. Fine. These things happen. We are all sinners, but we are supposed to make up for it. If you harbor anger it will only grow stronger." But his children were not interested in listening to an old man. They thought he sounded addled. Besides, Ivan had no interest in humbling himself before his neighbor.

"I never pulled his beard," Ivan said, when he heard of the hair on its way to the district court. "He pulled the hair out himself."

"In fact, Gabriel's son grabbed at my shirt yesterday and tore off the buttons. Just look at it!" he screamed. Then Ivan, too, took off for the district court.

Meanwhile, not a day went by when some small, fresh infraction did not occur between the longstanding neighbors. They quarreled about every little thing. Even the young children abused each other, having learned how by watching their elders. When the women met by the riverside, which was almost a daily occurrence as they rinsed the family clothes, every word shared between them turned from friendliness and familiarity to nagging and bitterness.

As time passed from the original incident of the hen's egg, these once good neighbors slandered each other almost daily. After a year, the suits and countersuits between Ivan and Gabriel in the district court, and before the justice of the peace, were thrown out by exhausted judges. Only the grandfather lying on top of the stove could see what was happening. He kept urging his family, again and again, "What are you doing? Stop all of this payback! Keep to your own work, your own affairs, and bear no grudge against another. The more you indulge your anger without checking it against your better inclinations, the worse off we all will be." But no one was listening.

THREE

Seven years went by. The grandfather grew older and more tired, and the families of Ivan and Gabriel came to live in a kind of quiet bitterness. Still neighbors, they were occasionally in the same place at the same time, and on every occasion the town held its collective breath, desperately hoping that all would go well.

One evening, at a community wedding, both families were present. Both Ivan and Gabriel were drinking a great deal, as men are prone to do at weddings, particularly when their enemies are present. As new wine was poured into pitchers upon the tables, Ivan's daughter-in-law could be heard saying to those at her table, "Gabriel over there stole a horse last week. I saw it with my own eyes." Each person whispered it to the one beside him or her until it reached Gabriel's own ears.

Gabriel was drunk, but not drunk enough. So when someone pointed to the daughter-in-law as the person who began the tale, Gabriel sprang from his chair, filled with rage, and gave the woman such a blow to the side of her head that she hit the floor with a thud. To make matters worse, she was pregnant; everyone knew that she was. What did Ivan do? He was delighted. "Finally, I can get rid of this man! Surely, he's off to Siberia now," he said.

The following morning, before dawn, Ivan arrived at his local councilor's house to lodge a complaint. He could barely contain his outrage. The councilor followed Ivan back to the house to examine the daughter-in-law. But since she was up and around, chasing the hens across the yard, the councilor promptly dismissed the case. Ivan was still angry, and undeterred. Storming from his yard, leaving the councilor standing among the chickens, Ivan called out, "I'm going to the district court!"

Seven years had gone by since the earlier round of court cases, and Ivan had made many friends among the clerks of the court. He brought with him a jug of vodka, and within three-quarters of an hour, Ivan had his neighbor, Gabriel, sentenced to a flogging. "Twenty lashes with a birch rod two weeks from today," the secretary clerk read out the following day in town for all to hear. Gabriel was there to hear the sentence, and he went white as a sheet.

Two days later, the judge of the district court reviewed the case and sent word to Ivan and Gabriel to come to his chambers.

"Look here, men," he said, "I have reviewed this case, as well as the dozens of cases filed by the two of you over the years against each other. Here's what I think: You need to reconcile between yourselves."

One of the judge's clerks, hearing this, piped up, "But a decision has been rendered, sir. It must be executed."

"Be still!" the judge shot back at his clerk. "The first of all laws is to obey God, and God loves peace." Then the judge began to try to persuade the peasants to talk and resolve their differences. "No one should need a flogging," he said after a while. "This has gone too far."

"I will never ask for his forgiveness," Gabriel said to the judge, his voice quivering, refusing even to look at Ivan.

"Neither will I!" Ivan spat.

FOUR

Ivan and Gabriel lived seven miles from the District Court. It was late in the afternoon by the time they made it home.

Ivan harnessed his horse and walked into his cottage. No one was home. His people were all still out in the fields. So he sat down in the kitchen and began to think. Ivan began to imagine what it would be like to be flogged, and he shuddered just a little. His heart grew heavy thinking of his old friend Gabriel and what lay in store for him.

Just then, someone coughed from atop the stove and Ivan turned to see his father. The older man pulled himself up and slid down. Leaning against the table where Ivan was seated, the grandfather asked, "So, has Gabriel been convicted?"

"Yes," Ivan replied. "Twenty lashes."

The old man shook his head. "A bad business, all of it," he said. "What good will flogging Gabriel do for you?"

"He won't do it again," Ivan replied.

"You can't see, my son," the father began. "You are blinded by malice. Sure, he has acted badly, but so have you. Such enmity exists only when there are two sides producing it. This is not how his father and I used to live beside each other. We lived as neighbors should. We helped each other. We opened our doors to each other.

"Think of your soul, son. Gabriel says a bad word to you and you respond with two. He hits you and you hit back twice. No! Jesus, when he walked the earth, taught us fools something very different from all of that. If you get a sharp word from anyone, keep silent and his own conscience will accuse him. That is what Christ taught. If you get slapped, offer the other cheek. Again, his conscience will rebuke him. He will soften, and listen. That's the way." Ivan was silent, listening. Then his father sat down again.

After a while, the grandfather spoke up once more. "Hear me, son. Go back to the district court and put an end to this. Make up with Gabriel, in God's name, and invite him to our house. Prepare tea. Have a bottle of vodka handy. Put an end to this wicked business."

He's right, Ivan thought to himself.

"Put out the fire before it spreads any further," the grandfather concluded.

Ivan didn't, but he pondered his father's words as he headed out to the pasture to feed the cattle that night.

FIVE

As Ivan opened the gate to the pasture, he heard on the other side of the fence his neighbor Gabriel cursing. Bitterness toward Gabriel rose quietly again in his heart, and Ivan returned to the house.

There he found his wife preparing supper, his eldest son making strips to repair shoes, his daughter-in-law pausing over a book, and another son preparing to go out to pasture the horses for the night. Everything seemed pleasant and bright inside, except for how Ivan felt toward his neighbor.

As Ivan entered that bright room where his family were all going about their business, he felt gloomy and angry. Tossing the cat from a chair, he sat down, only to jump back up again a few seconds later. Ivan couldn't get the image of Gabriel, nor the anger that consumed him, from his mind and heart. He walked back outside, onto the porch. Soon it was as dark as it could be. A moonless night.

Ivan began to walk stealthily around his property, checking to see what was missing, who was about, and wondering what mischief Gabriel and his family were up to. As he reached the fence he thought he saw a flicker of light, and then a quick flare that vanished in a split second. *Gabriel!* Ivan imagined.

Gabriel, meanwhile, was at that same moment walking on the other side of the fence, ruminating on the insult that Ivan was bringing down upon him. Moving stealthily, Gabriel paused at the precise moment that Ivan paused, also silently, on the other side. At that moment, Gabriel also thought he saw a flicker and a flare, but both vanished in a heartbeat. *What was that?* Gabriel thought.

Each man was carrying a box of matches in his coat, and a minute later, each thought they saw the image of the other before their eyes, doing something evil. The night was very dark. No one could see properly. Simultaneously, Ivan and Gabriel struck matches, pulled quickly from their breast pockets, setting fire to straw on the other's side of the fence. "Aha! Take that!" or something to that effect, they screamed in each other's direction. Within minutes, both their houses were in flames, the fire rising in quiet waves to the sky. Wives and children were screaming, running like animals from fiery dens. Ivan's youngest son barely managed to save his old grandfather.

*Within minutes, both their houses were in flames, the fire rising in
quiet waves to the sky.*

Fifteen minutes later all of Ivan's and Gabriel's neighbors were also fleeing their homes carrying what belongings they could. The fire spread more rapidly than any fire anyone had ever witnessed in town, engulfing half the village, lasting all night long—until it finally burnt out at morning light, exhausted of its own power.

SIX

Ivan was still standing staring at the embers of his fallen roof when a village elder came to find him.

"Ivan, your father is dying!" he said. "He sent me for you."

Ivan followed the elder to his cottage on the other side of the village. There, someone had taken Ivan's father during the commotion of the night before. When Ivan entered, he saw his father lying on a bench holding a candle; the priest had come and administered the final rites. His father stirred a little when Ivan entered the cottage, but the old man could not sit up. Ivan knelt on one knee and put his right ear up to his father's mouth.

"What did I tell you, Ivan?" the grandfather whispered. "Who has burned down everything you own, in fact, our entire village?"

"It was *him*, father! I saw him. . . . "

"No, Ivan. Who brought all of this destruction down upon you?"

And at that moment, Ivan saw clearly.

"Yes," the old man said. "Always quench a fire at the first spark, my boy. Don't you know it can bring down the house?"

And then the grandfather died.

THEN PETER CAME UP AND SAID TO HIM,

"LORD, HOW OFTEN WILL MY BROTHER SIN AGAINST ME,

AND I FORGIVE HIM? AS MANY AS SEVEN TIMES?" JESUS SAID TO HIM,

"I DO NOT SAY TO YOU SEVEN TIMES, BUT SEVENTY TIMES SEVEN."

MATTHEW 18:21–22 ESV

<small>⟨⟩</small> AUTHOR'S NOTES <small>⟨⟩</small>

THREE SIMPLE MEN

Tolstoy's folktale was first published in 1886 and titled "The Three Hermits." "It is a typically subversive work," writes one of his biographers.[6] Why? The story illustrates Tolstoy's spiritual battles with the Orthodox Church, the state religion of Russia. In both his fiction and nonfiction, Tolstoy was always exploring the question of where spiritual wisdom and truth reside, in the Church or in the humble, simple life of the peasants, and he always turned to the latter.[7] I have removed some of this tension in order to remove the tale from the exclusive provenance of Tolstoy's biography, thereby universalizing it for the twenty-first century, non-Russian reader. So, in my version, the three men are not necessarily monks, mendicants, or hermits (you'll encounter all three nouns in other versions of this story), but are simply "simple" and "little," in accord with the teachings of Jesus in the Gospels.

One biographical detail is essential: The legend of "The Three Elders" preceded Tolstoy's tale. Tolstoy heard the story of three raw, pious men on a remote island from a peasant storyteller and immediately recognized similarities between the setting and a true incident from the life of one of his ancestors, Pyotr Andreyevich Tolstoy (1645–1729). A favorite ambassador of the tsar, Pyotr fell out of royal favor late in life and was imprisoned by the tsar in an island monastery-turned-prison near the Arctic Circle, where the Northern Dvina River flows into the White Sea. There, Pyotr died. For centuries, that Russian Orthodox monastery, Solovski in Tolstoy's tale, was a place of pilgrimage for Russians. Pilgrimage to monasteries was to Russian Orthodox Christians what pilgrimage to places like Compostela and Canterbury was to Christians throughout Western Europe. Ironically, Solovski became a gulag concentration camp after the Russian Revolution of 1917,[8] and today it is a major tourist attraction, mostly for Russians.

The primary liberty I have taken in my version of the folktale is to create characters out of the three simple men before the action takes place. The first line of Tolstoy's version, which varies according to English translations, is: "A bishop set sail in a ship from the city of Archangel [English for 'Arkhangelsk'] to Solovki." Instead, I set the scene by describing the men.

The Scripture quotation at the end of the tale, from Matthew 18:21–22, was important to Tolstoy. He also uses it as the first of

four passages from the Gospels at the beginning of his 1899 novel
Resurrection.

A GODSON LEARNS TO FIGHT EVIL

I have greatly simplified this tale, reducing it to approximately
two-thirds the length that it is in Tolstoy's rendering. In so doing,
I've removed some of Tolstoy's preachiness, as well as some of the
more magical elements of the story that have the main character
observing creatures in nature playing out actions and destinies
mirroring those of the human actors. I felt those scenes detracted
from the power of the kernel of what is most important. Still, the
magical first part of the tale remains, and I leave it to the reader to
ponder why it is important that the godson's Christian origins are
shrouded in mystery.

Tolstoy was simultaneously crafting folktales and didactic prose
works in the 1880s, and, as I write in the introduction, his tales are
always more powerful when they don't try so hard to instruct, as in
the prose works, such as *What I Believe* (1884) and *The Kingdom of
God Is Within You* (1893). Those books, which had a powerful effect

in their time, were inspired in large part by Tolstoy's dedication to the teaching of Christ in Matthew 5:29, "Resist not an evil person," as is this story. *What I Believe* was in fact banned throughout Russia because, as Tolstoy remembers, "When giving an account of my belief in Christ's teaching I could not avoid a statement of why I disbelieve, and regard as erroneous, the Church doctrine which is usually called Christianity."[9] In contrast, his short tales don't usually criticize the Church directly—only indirectly.

ONE NEGLECTED SPARK MAY BURN DOWN A HOUSE

If you don't read this story and laugh at least a little, it hasn't succeeded. The extravagance of the bitterness between the two families is meant to show the absurdity of human nature.

The story was first published by Tolstoy in 1885. The most important but subtle change in my version was to make the grandfather, ill with asthma and lying on top of the stove, more central. I wanted his character to function almost like the water pitcher I once saw in a Chekhov play that was a touchstone for all the action, something (or someone) to which everyone keeps returning for perspective. An elderly man lying on a house stove is, in fact, a frequent fixture in Tolstoy's stories, and was common in nineteenth-century Russia in general. In this tale, the aging, perpetually ill grandfather is the focal point of wisdom. The same is true in Tolstoy's "Three Deaths," a story from 1859.

To properly understand the setting, one must imagine a stove that looks nothing like the ranges or fireplaces of most Western households. The stove in a nineteenth-century Russian hut usually filled about one full quarter of the home, and included cooking spaces as well as facilities to heat the house. Ledges and shelves, plus rich ambient heat, offered many opportunities for sitting and lying comfortably upon them, particularly for those recuperating from illness or injury.

ENDNOTES

1   Leo Tolstoy, *Tolstoy's Letters: 1880-1910*, ed. and trans. R. F. Christian (New York: Charles Scribner's Sons, 1978), 2:395. This is a famously long missive in which Leo attempts to justify his recent religious commitments to his wife, Sonya, who sees them impinging upon the happiness of their marriage, home, and family. It ends as follows, including the final, unfinished sentence: "A struggle to the death is going on between us. Either God's works, or not God's works. And since God is within you . . ." (Ibid., 399).

2   Brian Attebery, *Stories about Stories: Fantasy and the Remaking of Myth* (New York: Oxford University Press), 4.

3   Journal entry of March 12, 1870, quoted in Henri Troyat, *Tolstoy*, trans. Nancy Amphoux (New York: Penguin Books, 1970), 524.

4   Unmailed letter written to L. Y. Obolensky, April 1885; see *Tolstoy's Letters*, 381.

5   Philip Pullman, *Fairy Tales from the Brothers Grimm: A New English Version* (New York: Penguin, 2013), xiii.

6   Rosamund Bartlett, *Tolstoy: A Russian Life* (London: Profile Books, 2013), 17.

7   Most notably, Tolstoy's *What I Believe* was published in 1884, two years before this tale, and stated in no uncertain terms the famous novelist's split with the teachings of the Orthodox Church.

8   Bartlett, *Tolstoy*, 14–18.

9   Leo Tolstoy, *The Kingdom of God and Peace Essays*, trans. Alymer Maude (New York: Oxford University Press, 1946), 1.